D0978815

Pony-Crazed Princess

Princess Ellie's Royal Jamboree

by Diana Kimpton

Illustrated by Lizzie Finlay

Hyperion Paperbacks for Children / New York

AN IMPRINT OF DISNEY BOOK GROUP

In memory of my mum,
who always made holidays special
—LF

First published in the United Kingdom in 2005 as
The Pony-Mad Princess: Princess Ellie's Christmas
by Usborne Publishing Ltd.
Based on an original concept by Anne Finnis

Printed in the United States of America

First U.S. edition, 2008

1 3 5 7 9 10 8 6 4 2

This book is set in 14.5-point Nadine Normal.

ISBN 978-1-4231-1531-1

Visit www.hyperionbooksforchildren.com

Chapter 1

"Ouch!" said Princess Ellie as she stabbed herself with the needle. She sucked her sore finger and stared pleadingly at her governess. "Can I please stop sewing now? I want to go to the stable."

"You always do," replied Miss Stringle. "But your ponies will have to wait. You need to finish your mother's present. The Royal Jamboree is the day after tomorrow."

Ellie didn't need reminding. She had been looking forward to the Jamboree for weeks. And she felt as if she'd been sewing for almost as long. But at least it was better than schoolwork, especially since she could do it in the ruby sitting room instead of the classroom.

She leaned back in the red velvet armchair and looked at her work. The cross-stitched crown looked lopsided. "Are you sure Mom wants an embroidered handkerchief?" she asked. "I could have ordered her something much nicer from a catalog." She knew there was no point in suggesting that she could have bought something in a store. Princesses didn't go shopping.

"I've told you before," declared Miss Stringle, "the Queen can buy anything she wants, whenever she wants it. So buying her a Jamboree present isn't special. It's much more thoughtful to make her one."

"I made presents for my mother when I was a girl," said Great-Aunt Edwina, who was sitting nearby on another red velvet chair. "The Royal Jamboree has always been one of my favorite holidays."

"Mine, too," said Ellie, as she started to sew again. "I can't wait to open all those presents piled in the ballroom."

Miss Stringle gave her a disapproving stare. "I am disappointed to hear that,

Princess Aurelia. The Royal Jamboree is supposed to be about giving, not receiving. The whole point of the celebration is to remind everyone in the kingdom about the importance of kindness. Don't forget the story of the squirrels."

"I know, I know," said Ellie. Ever since she was little, she had loved the story of the two little princes who got lost in the snowy woods overnight; according to the story, they were saved by a family of red squirrels who gave them nuts to eat and snuggled up close to them to keep them warm.

"Nowadays it seems more about having a day off from work and eating too much," grumbled Great-Aunt Edwina. "Royal Jamborees were much better when I was a girl."

"Did it snow then?" asked Ellie.

The old lady shook her head. "Not that I can remember. But it did when the princes were lost. It must have been so cold in the forest that night."

"And so beautiful," sighed Ellie, who had seen snow for the first time in her life when she went on vacation with her parents to Andirovia. "Just imagine the moon glistening on the snow-covered trees. It would be wonderful if it snowed for this year's Jamboree."

"That is highly unlikely," snorted Miss Stringle. "The princes got lost four hundred years ago. The climate was much colder then. We rarely have snow at all anymore."

"But this year is going to be different," declared Ellie. "Kate's grandmother told me to make a wish when I stirred the nuts into the Jamboree pudding mix. And I wished for snow on this Royal Jamboree—just like there was on the very first one. It will make the day absolutely perfect."

Miss Stringle shook her head and sighed. "I'm afraid no amount of wishing will make it snow. No matter what the palace cook believes, there is nothing in a pudding mix that can change the weather."

Ellie didn't want to believe her. Surely wishes came true sometimes. She glanced hopefully out of the window. But the sky was clear and blue. There were no clouds in sight.

Great-Aunt Edwina didn't seem to notice

Ellie's disappointment. She was busy remembering past Royal Jamboree celebrations. "We always had a wonderful feast when I was a girl."

"We still do," said Ellie. "Kate's grandmother has a fantastic roast planned." She sewed the last stitch on the handkerchief and handed it to Miss Stringle. "I'm finished. Please, may I go?"

But to Ellie's dismay, her governess produced another handkerchief. "I thought you could do one for Kate, as well. It could have a horseshoe instead of a crown."

Ellie stared at her in horror. "Kate's my best friend! I want to

give her something she'll really, really enjoy. And anyway, she doesn't even use hankies—she only uses tissues." Just then, she spotted the mailman's van through the window and added, "Besides, I've already ordered her the perfect present. That must be it arriving now."

She raced out of the room and reached the front door at the same time as the mailman. Higginbottom, the butler, took the bulging bag of mail from him and tipped the contents out onto a table. There were a few postcards, several boring-looking brown envelopes, and two small parcels.

"Which one's mine?" squealed Ellie, hopping up and down with excitement.

"Neither of them," said Higginbottom. "They're both for His Majesty."

“You must be wrong!” cried Ellie. “Kate’s present is supposed to come today.” She picked up the bag and turned it inside out. But there was no sign of the missing parcel. “What am I going to do?” she groaned.

“Now, don’t panic,” said Higginbottom. “There’s another delivery tomorrow morning. That’s the last one before the Royal Jamboree.”

His words made Ellie feel slightly better. The next day was the day before the Jamboree, so if the parcel arrived then, she would still be able to give Kate the perfect present. But if it didn’t come, she’d have nothing at all to give her best friend.

Chapter 2

Ellie burst out laughing when she arrived at the stable and found Meg, the palace groom, wearing a pair of tufty squirrel's ears. "I'm just getting into the Royal Jamboree mood," Meg explained.

"Look at me," cried Kate, as she came out of Angel's stable. "Meg's got us some, too." The squirrel's ears sticking out of her long, straight hair waggled as she walked.

"Here are yours," said Meg, holding out an identical pair attached to a green head-band.

"Thanks," said Ellie. "They're great." She took off her crown and put on the ears. Then she tried to balance the crown in its usual place. But it wouldn't fit. The ears were too close together, so there wasn't room for the crown as well. "Darn!" she said.

"Couldn't you leave your crown off just this once?" said Meg.

Ellie shook her head. "I'll get into trouble if I'm caught. I'm only allowed to take it off when I put on my riding hat or my tiara." Wearing a crown all the time was one of the annoying parts of being a princess.

"I've got an idea," laughed Kate. She ran over and took the crown. Then she stuffed it on Ellie's head with one of the squirrel's ears poking through the middle of it.

Ellie ran into the tack room and stared at herself in the mirror. "That looks really silly," she giggled as she pulled off the crown. Reluctantly she took off the ears and put them on the table. Then she put on her riding hat and said, "Come on, let's go for a ride."

"Can I take Rainbow?" asked Kate. Although Angel was Kate's pony, she was only a foal, still too young to be ridden.

"Of course you can," said Ellie. She knew immediately which pony she wanted to ride. Shadow, the Shetland, was too small for her, and she'd ridden Moonbeam the day before. Starlight was Angel's mom and needed to stay at home with her foal. So it was obviously Sundance's turn.

The chestnut pony seemed as pleased to be going out as Ellie was. He whickered a welcome as she went into the stable. Then he lowered his head to make it easy for her to put on his bridle, opening his mouth to let her gently slide the bit between his teeth.

As soon as he was ready, Ellie led him outside, tightened his girth, and swung herself onto his saddle. She waited until Kate was settled on Rainbow. Then they rode together out of the yard and up a lane that took them into the palace grounds.

"I wonder if the ponies can tell the Royal Jamboree's coming up," said Ellie as she turned Sundance through an open gate into the deer park. The chestnut pony tossed his head and started to trot as soon as he felt the grass beneath his feet.

"They are very excited!" yelled Kate as she struggled to keep Rainbow under control. The gray pony was pulling on the reins, trying to go faster.

"They've got too much energy," laughed Ellie. "Let's use some of it up." She urged Sundance into a canter and then a gallop. Faster and faster they went, until Ellie felt she was almost flying. The wind whistled through her hair as she leaned forward over his neck.

Sundance raced across the deer park with Rainbow close behind. As they neared the forest on the other side, Ellie felt the chestnut pony start to tire. She slowed him to a walk and turned in among the trees, onto a path that sloped gently uphill. It was just wide enough for her and Kate to ride side by side.

Rainbow and Sundance didn't try to trot anymore. They were happy to walk slowly through the sunlight that dappled the

branches. Their hooves scrunched on the soft ground, and their ears flicked back and forth as they listened to the sounds of the woods.

Ellie leaned forward and patted Sundance's neck. "They're both much calmer now," she said to Kate. "But *I'm* still as excited as I was before."

"So am I," agreed Kate. "I can hardly wait until tomorrow. Mom and Dad should be here by ten. I'm not going to bed until they've arrived." Kate didn't see her parents very often, because they worked abroad. While they traveled around the world, she stayed with her grandparents at the palace, so that she could go to school.

"Have you told them you're going to be on TV?"

"Of course I have," said Kate. "They were really surprised. They could hardly believe your parents want everyone in the palace to be in their program."

"They always do," replied Ellie. The Jamboree TV broadcast was a royal tradition. Every year, the King gave a speech to all the people in the kingdom. He liked to wish them a Happy Jamboree and give them a brief look at the royal celebrations.

Kate ducked to avoid a low branch. "I've never been on TV before. I hope I don't do anything wrong."

"You'll be fine," said Ellie. "Anyway, there's a rehearsal tomorrow morning, so you'll have a chance to practice."

She shortened Sundance's reins and pushed him into a trot. "Come on. Let's do some jumping." Kate urged Rainbow to go faster, and soon both ponies were leaping over the logs that lay across the path.

As they rode out of the trees onto the

open hillside, Ellie looked down at the palace below. There was still no sign of the snow she'd wished for. Perhaps that would come tomorrow, like Kate's present.

Chapter 3

To Ellie's disappointment, the last day before the Royal Jamboree dawned bright and sunny, without a hint of snow. She was drinking her breakfast orange juice from a crystal glass when Higginbottom came into the dining room. He bowed politely to the King and Queen and announced, "The TV crew has arrived, Your Majesties. They're just unloading their equipment."

"Good. I have to talk to the director," said the King. He gulped the last of his coffee and strode out of the room. Ellie followed him. She loved watching TV crews at work and knew it would be more fun than eating her toast.

The hall was busy with men carrying cameras, lights, and large rolls of cable. In the middle of them stood a woman wearing black pants and a purple silk shirt embroidered with scarlet dragons. Her hair was even curlier than Ellie's, but much shorter. It was dyed purple to match her top.

The woman gave the faintest hint of a curtsy and announced, "I'm Gloria Doria, your new director."

"What happened to the old one?" asked the King.

"He's sick in bed," replied Gloria. "So you've got me instead."

"I hope you know what you're doing," said the King, as he made his way toward the ballroom. "The Jamboree broadcast is very important to the Queen and me. We want it to be perfect."

Gloria scurried after him. "Don't worry. I'm one of the top directors in the country. I do all the Albert Blonde movies."

"Wow!" said Ellie. She loved watching Albert Blonde, secret agent, save the world from disaster. The special effects in those movies were spectacular.

So was the Royal Jamboree centerpiece in the ballroom. The enormous scale model of the palace was so tall that it almost touched the ceiling. Its windows were encrusted with jewels, its roof was covered in gleaming gold, and its towers and turrets were adorned with glittering multicolored lights. Piles of beautifully wrapped presents lay around the base of the model, waiting to be opened on Jamboree morning.

"That's pretty impressive," said Gloria Doria, looking at the model of the palace. "Does it do anything?"

The King looked surprised. "It's just a replica of the palace," he said. "What would you expect it to do?"

"Explode, perhaps?" suggested the director.

Ellie put her hand over her mouth to keep

from giggling. Gloria seemed to be having trouble leaving the world of Albert Blonde behind.

The King obviously thought the same. He raised his eyebrows and stared disapprovingly at Gloria. "Jamboree centerpieces do not explode. They do not revolve, and they do not bounce up and down. Is that understood?"

"Certainly, Your Majesty," replied the director. She looked serious, but the corners of her mouth twitched as if she were trying to hold back a smile.

The King lowered his eyebrows to their usual position and continued. "This is the perfect place for me to give my speech. The centerpiece will look good in the background."

"Will the entire royal family join you for the speech?" asked Gloria.

"And the staff." He glanced at his watch. "They'll all be here in a minute for the rehearsal."

As he spoke, a group of maids walked nervously into the ballroom. They looked flushed and excited at the prospect of being on TV. Ellie was pleased to see Kate arrive next. Her grandmother was with her. The flour on her apron suggested that she had been baking right up until the last minute.

While the TV crew set up the cameras, Gloria organized everyone into a group around the Jamboree centerpiece. Great-Aunt Edwina had a chair because she was old, while the King and Queen sat in their thrones. Gloria made Ellie and Kate sit on the floor in the front. "The viewers love to see children at the Jamboree," she explained.

When everyone was ready, Gloria clapped her hands and shouted, "Action!" Immediately, everyone went quiet except the King. He stood up and started his speech.

Ellie enjoyed listening to it the first time, but Gloria wasn't satisfied. She made him say it over and over again while she adjusted camera angles and microphones to make it all look perfect on TV.

Finally, she stepped back and sighed. "I'm afraid it's still not right, Your Majesty." She hesitated for a moment. Then she added, "It's just not interesting enough."

"I've spent hours writing that speech," complained the King. "I'm sure the usual director would have liked it."

Gloria smiled apologetically. "It's not the words that are the problem, Your Majesty. It's the image. We need some more action—something fun for the viewers to watch."

The King looked at her suspiciously. "I hope you don't want me to do anything silly."

"Of course not," replied Gloria. "What we need is something that looks more like a celebration."

"I've baked some squirrel-shaped gingerbread cookies," suggested Kate's grandmother. "We could eat those."

"I'm sure the viewers don't want to see us munching," replied the Queen.

"Maybe they'd be more interested in seeing us exchange presents," said Ellie.

"That's a brilliant idea!" cried Gloria. She

grabbed a parcel wrapped in purple paper and read out the label. *"To my very best friend, Ellie. With love from Kate."*

Kate blushed. "That's mine," she admitted. Then she turned to Ellie and whispered, "You weren't supposed to see it until tomorrow."

Gloria helped Kate to her feet and handed her the parcel. "Now, you stand here, and give your present to Ellie."

"You mean, Princess Aurelia," said Miss Stringle from the back of the crowd.

Gloria sighed and shrugged her shoulders. "Okay, Princess Aurelia it is." She turned to Ellie and added, "Okay, sweetie. You're up."

Ellie heard a sharp intake of breath from the direction of Miss Stringle. Her governess obviously did not approve of a princess being called "sweetie." But Ellie did. The more she saw of Gloria Doria, the more she liked her.

The director moved the girls around to find the best position for the camera. "Remember, this is just a rehearsal," she said.

"You can't open the present until we do it for real, tomorrow." Then she called "Action!" again.

"Hope you like it!" said Kate as she thrust the present into Ellie's hands.

Although they were only pretending, Ellie felt a thrill of excitement. It was such a beautiful parcel that she couldn't resist feeling it. Whatever was inside was very soft.

"That's brilliant," said Gloria. She pointed at Ellie and added, "Now, you give your present to Kate."

Ellie stared back at the director in horror and then looked back at Kate. How could she tell her best friend that she didn't have a present for her yet?

Chapter 4

There was a long pause while Ellie wondered desperately what to do. Then she had an idea.

"It isn't here," she announced. "I haven't wrapped it yet." She didn't explain that she didn't yet have anything to wrap.

Luckily, Gloria Doria didn't pursue the matter. "We don't really need to practice that part now."

Kate's grandmother looked anxiously at her watch. "I really need to get back to my baking."

The Queen nodded. "I think we've rehearsed enough. All the staff have a great deal to do today."

As the crowd broke up, Ellie spotted the mailman's van through the window. "Wait for me here," she told Kate. She slipped quietly out of the room and raced to the hall.

The mailbag was sitting on the table, waiting for Higginbottom to sort it. But there was no sign of the butler. Ellie was too impatient to wait for him, so she grabbed the bag herself and spilled its contents out. Envelopes shot in all directions. Some of them slid across the shiny table and fell onto the floor.

She didn't bother to pick them up. She wasn't looking for letters or postcards. She was only interested in parcels, and she hadn't seen any yet. Ellie shook the bag again. There was still something in there, but it wouldn't come out.

She peered inside, but it was too dark in the bag to see anything. So she reached inside, pushing her hand right to the bottom. Her fingers felt a single parcel. She pulled it free, hoping desperately that it was the one she was waiting for. If it wasn't, she knew she would cry.

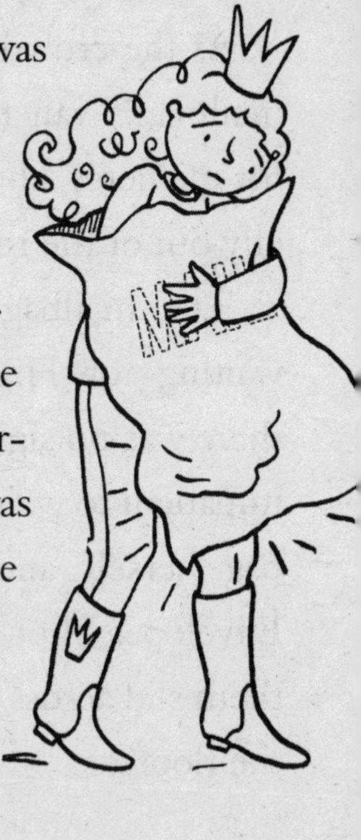

To her relief, the parcel had *Princess Aurelia*

written on it in large letters. Next to the address was a label announcing that it had come from

Pony Tails magazine. That was where she'd ordered Kate's present from. At long last, here was the parcel she'd been waiting for.

There wasn't time to open it now, because Kate was waiting for her in the ballroom. If Ellie took too long, she might come looking for her and see the parcel. Then it wouldn't be a surprise.

Ellie knew she needed to hide it until later. So she ran into the ruby sitting room and slid the parcel under the chair. She was sure no one would see it there.

She ran back to the ballroom feeling much calmer. She had the perfect present for her best friend. Now she just needed some snow to make the Royal Jamboree complete.

Kate was waiting for her beside the huge centerpiece. The King and Queen, along with the palace servants, had already left. But the TV crew was still there, busy finalizing the arrangements for the broadcast.

The chief cameraman walked up to Gloria Doria with a gloomy expression on his face. "I don't like the way it finishes," he said. "It just fizzles out."

"I know," agreed Gloria. "It needs something really special to happen at the end."

"How about making the centerpiece explode?" suggested the cameraman. "The special effects team could rig it with fireworks."

Ellie couldn't resist interrupting. "I don't

think Dad would like that," she giggled.

"Neither do I," laughed Gloria. "Anyway, fireworks wouldn't look right. We need something cuter, like bluebirds, or butterflies, or . . ."

". . . Squirrels?" suggested Ellie.

"That's a fantastic idea," said Gloria. "Perhaps we could have some performing squirrels come in at the end."

"You'll never find any of those on such short notice," said the cameraman, who seemed to enjoy being gloomy. "Plus, it's very hard to train squirrels. They've got a mind of their own."

"Just one would be enough, and it doesn't have to be a real one," said Gloria thoughtfully. "We're sure to have a squirrel costume in the wardrobe department. Someone dressed up would be just as good."

"It might even be better," said Ellie, who wasn't at all sure that it was kind to make squirrels do tricks.

"I'm sure my granddad would do it!"

cried Kate. "He enjoyed dressing up as a pirate at the party on New Year's Eve."

"Great!" said Gloria, with a beaming smile. "Now, we've just got to decide how to make his arrival look really dramatic."

"We could strap him to a wire and make it look as if he were flying," suggested the cameraman.

Gloria nodded approvingly. "That would look good. The special effects team is very good at making people fly."

Kate shook her head. "I don't think Grandma would approve of that. She'd be upset if there were an accident and he fell."

"I don't think he'd be very pleased, either," said Ellie. "Couldn't he arrive in a fancy car?"

"Cars are huge," moaned the cameraman.

"You'll never get one in here, unless those French windows open really wide."

"They do," said Kate. "Ellie and I rode the ponies through them on the day Angel was born."

"Well, that problem's solved," said Gloria. "Though I'm not sure that a car is right for a squirrel. If only there were something else Kate's grandfather could travel in—something more connected with the countryside."

Ellie squealed with excitement. "I know just the thing!" she said.

Chapter 5

"You could use Shadow, my Shetland pony," explained Ellie. "He pulls a carriage that would be perfect for the broadcast." She grabbed Gloria by the hand and pulled her toward the door. "Come on. I'll show you."

"You'll love him," added Kate, tugging on the director's other hand.

"Okay, okay," laughed Gloria. "Let's go. This could be just what we need."

When they arrived at the stable, they found Great-Aunt Edwina leaning over Shadow's door. "I've come to see my favorite pony," she said, smiling.

"So have we," said Ellie. She got Shadow's halter and led the black Shetland pony out into the yard.

"Isn't she sweet!" cooed Gloria. "Just look at that gorgeous mane and those teeny, tiny hooves."

"You'll love his carriage, too," said Ellie.

But Gloria looked disappointed when Meg pulled it out of the barn. "It looks very dull. I thought royal carriages were always gold or silver."

"You're thinking of Cinderella's coach," said Kate.

"*That* would be perfect," sighed Gloria. "But I don't have a pumpkin or a magic wand to conjure one up. So I'll have to ask the special effects team to brighten up your carriage instead."

"We can do that!" cried Ellie, her eyes shining with excitement. "I'm great with arts and crafts."

"So am I," declared Kate. "By the time we're finished, it will be perfect for the Jamboree broadcast."

"So, that's what you're up to," said Great-Aunt Edwina, as she gave Shadow a peppermint. He crunched it happily and nuzzled her pocket in search of another one. "I hope you have someone who is good at driving ponies."

Kate's mouth dropped open with dismay. "Oh, no!" she groaned. "Granddad has never driven a carriage before."

Ellie sighed. "It was a good idea while it lasted." Then she remembered how much her great-aunt enjoyed driving Shadow. "I don't suppose you'd like to help?" she asked.

"Of course I would," declared the old lady, "provided I don't have to dress up in a silly costume."

"I'm sure we can find you something nice to wear," smiled Gloria. "We brought loads of outfits with us, just in case." She held her hands in front of her face, pretending they were a camera, and peered through them at Shadow. "It's going to look wonderful when this little fellow trots into the ballroom."

"It will look even better if it snows," said Ellie, as she pictured the perfect scene in her imagination.

Gloria laughed. "That would be great. But

I don't think it's very likely—not with our climate."

"You might be surprised," said Ellie. "I made a wish that it would snow at this year's Jamboree."

"And she was stirring the Jamboree pudding when she did it," explained Kate. "Grandma says that makes wishes more likely to come true."

"Well, whatever the weather, let's keep our plan a secret," suggested Gloria. "We want this to be a complete surprise." Then she whisked Great-Aunt Edwina away to choose her clothes.

The girls set to work immediately on the carriage. They polished all the woodwork and brushed the dust off the velvet cushions. Then they got saddle soap and metal polish from the tack room and cleaned Shadow's harness until it gleamed.

All that work made them hungry, so they were delighted when a footman arrived with a silver tray piled with food. "The Queen thought you might like your lunch at the stable as a special treat," he explained.

As they sat in the tack room munching on peanut butter sandwiches and tea, Ellie wondered whether she should try to slip away to wrap Kate's present. But there was still so much to do to the carriage that there wasn't any time to spare. She was sure the parcel would be safe in its hiding place. She could leave it there until the evening and wrap it after dinner.

Just as they finished eating, the chief cameraman arrived with a large box. It was packed with shiny decorations. There were garlands of silver leaves, silver bells that tinkled as they moved, and hundreds of silver star stickers.

Ellie and Kate carefully peeled off the stars one by one and stuck them on the sides of the carriage. They wound the garlands of silver leaves around the long shafts until they couldn't see the wood at all. Then they tied more leaves onto the straps of Shadow's harness. As they worked, they became more and more excited.

Meg looked impressed when she came over to see how they were coming along. "That looks fantastic. Even Cinderella would be jealous."

"I'm dying to show it to Mom and Dad!" squealed Kate. "They must be on their way by now. I'm so looking forward to seeing them."

Ellie smiled and put her finger to her lips. "*Shhh!* Remember, it's a secret—you mustn't tell them what we're planning."

Then she turned to Meg and said, "Shadow's carriage will look even better when it's finished. We haven't even put the silver bells on yet."

Meg glanced at her watch and shook her head. "It's too late to do that now. It's almost dinnertime."

"I love those bells," sighed Kate, as they walked back to the palace. "It's a shame not to use them."

"We still can," said Ellie. "Let's go back this evening and put them on. I'll meet you at the stable at seven o'clock." She was sure that that would leave her plenty of time to collect the hidden parcel containing Kate's present and wrap it up.

As soon as she'd finished her meal, Ellie slipped into the ruby sitting room. She knelt down in front of the red velvet chair and reached underneath. But her searching fingers only found empty air. Kate's present had completely disappeared.

Chapter 6

Ellie slumped onto the sitting-room floor, feeling confused. Where could the parcel have gone?

"Is this what you're looking for?" asked a voice from behind her.

She turned around and saw Miss Stringle holding the missing package. Ellie was so pleased that she nearly kissed her. But she stopped herself just in time and asked,

"Where did you find it?"

Miss Stringle smiled. "I was playing chess with your great-aunt when the maids moved the chair to clean the carpet. I picked it up as soon as I saw that it was addressed to you." She shook the parcel gently. "Is it something important?"

"It's Kate's present," replied Ellie, as she ripped off the paper. "It's a T-shirt with a heart-shaped picture of Angel and the words *I love Angel* written on it in bright red letters."

The T-shirt was in a plastic bag, neatly folded. She pulled it out and held the shirt up for Miss Stringle to admire. "Do you like it? I took the photo myself."

Miss Stringle looked puzzled. "But I thought Angel was a foal?"

Ellie turned the T-shirt around and stared at it in dismay. The words were perfect, but the heart-shaped picture wasn't. Instead of Kate's skewbald foal, it showed a huge, fat cart-horse with one blue eye and one brown eye. He was much bigger than Angel and nowhere near as pretty.

"It's the wrong photo!" she wailed. "What am I going to do?"

"You'll have to send it back," said Miss Stringle. "It's their mistake, so I'm sure they'll replace it."

"But there isn't any time," groaned Ellie,

forcing back the tears that pricked at her eyes. "I won't have anything to give Kate at the Jamboree."

"Yes, you will," declared Miss Stringle. She handed Ellie a plain white handkerchief. "I'm sure you can embroider a horseshoe this evening, if you sew fast enough."

Ellie took it without enthusiasm. She still didn't want to give Kate a hankie with a horseshoe. But she didn't have a choice. It would be even worse to give nothing at all to her best friend.

She trudged up the spiral staircase to her bedroom and tipped the contents of her sewing box onto her quilt. The brightly colored embroidery threads looked much more cheerful than she felt. It was hard to choose the best one for Kate, but Ellie finally picked a shiny thread with gold strands twisted into it. Maybe that would make the hankie look special.

She soon wished she had made a different choice. The gold thread was stiffer than the ordinary ones and much harder to sew with. Each stitch took forever. She had completed only three by the time her pink alarm clock told her it was nearly seven. It was time to go to the stable to meet Kate.

Ellie dumped the sewing onto her bed. She'd have to finish it later.

As she ran through the palace, the excitement of the next day's Jamboree pushed away her disappointment about the present. Thousands of colorful streamers crisscrossed the ceilings, and strings of tiny silver squirrels scampered across the walls.

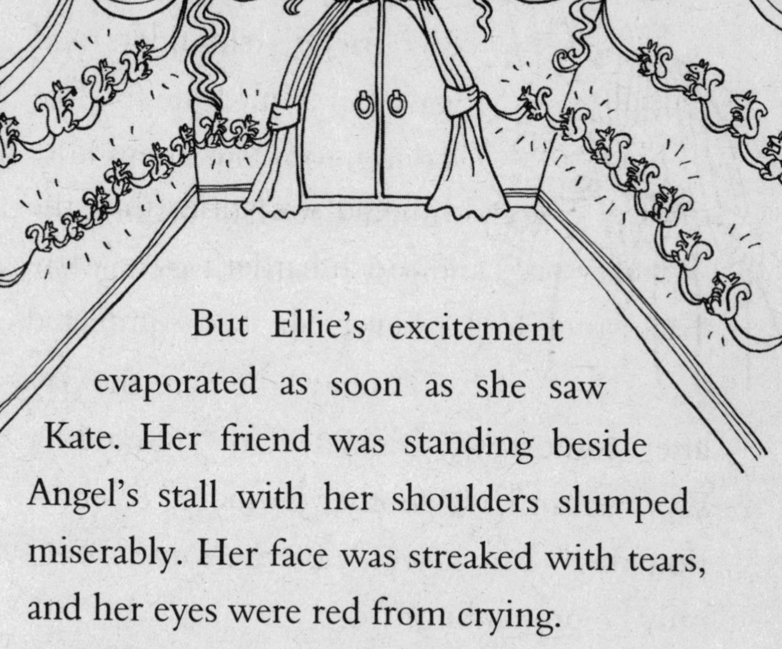

But Ellie's excitement evaporated as soon as she saw Kate. Her friend was standing beside Angel's stall with her shoulders slumped miserably. Her face was streaked with tears, and her eyes were red from crying.

"What's wrong?" asked Ellie.

"It's Mom and Dad," sobbed Kate. "Their car broke down on the way to the airport. They've missed the last plane home. There's no way they can make it here for the Jamboree."

Ellie put her arm around her friend's shoulders and gave her a hug. She felt like crying, too. She knew how much Kate had been looking forward to seeing her parents.

"They'll be here the day after tomorrow," sighed Kate. "Grandma says we can have another Jamboree celebration then. But it won't be the same. We'll only be pretending."

"I'm really sorry," said Ellie, trying to think of a way to cheer her friend up. Then she picked up the silver bells and waved them in Kate's face. "Let's put these on the carriage. It'll get us back in a happy mood."

Kate smiled weakly and started to tie the

bells on to the spokes of the wheels. Ellie set to work, too. It was a slow task, but it was the perfect finishing touch to make the carriage look beautiful.

Moonlight, Sundance, and Rainbow poked their heads out of their stalls to see what was happening. Shadow was so small that he couldn't put his head over the top of his door, so he banged it with his hooves to attract Ellie's attention.

She leaned over the door and gave him one of his favorite peppermints. "You're going to be the star of the show tomorrow."

"I hope he enjoys it more than I do," groaned Kate. "Everything's going wrong this year."

Ellie nodded in agreement. She so wanted this to be the best Royal Jamboree ever, but it was starting to look as if it might be the worst. Then, suddenly, she thought of a plan—one that could solve everything. But she couldn't do it on her own.

Chapter 7

Ellie knew there was no time to waste. If her plan was going to work, she had to ask for help as soon as possible.

"I've got to get back," she told Kate. "I've still got your present to wrap." She didn't mention that she hadn't made it yet.

She left her friend talking to Angel and ran back to the palace. There was no sign of her parents in the King's office, the Queen's study, or the ruby sitting room. She finally found them in the parlor, eating toasted marshmallows while they watched TV.

The King held out the dish. "Have one, Aurelia. They're delicious."

The sight of the sweets made Ellie's mouth water. Though she longed to take one, she decided against it. She had to stay focused on the task at hand. She couldn't let herself get distracted by marshmallows. So she resisted the temptation and announced, "I've got a terrific idea."

"Oh, dear," said the Queen, with a worried look on her face. Some of Ellie's previous ideas had turned out not to be as brilliant as she'd first thought.

"I hope it's not going to cause trouble," said the King. "We don't want anything to spoil the Jamboree."

"This won't," protested Ellie. "I promise." She explained her plan as quickly as she could.

The King looked doubtful. "It's a lovely

idea. I'm just not sure if it will work."

"I don't know if there's enough time," added the Queen, looking at her watch.

"Please try," begged Ellie. "Please, please, please."

To her relief, they finally agreed. The King made several phone calls. Then he summoned Higginbottom and told the butler about the important task they wanted him to do.

Once Ellie knew her plan was under way, she went back to her bedroom and resumed her sewing. She was still working on the hankie when the Queen came in to kiss her good night.

"Don't stay up too long," she said, as she gave Ellie a peck on the forehead. "You want to be well rested for the festivities tomorrow."

Ellie felt herself getting tired. But finishing Kate's present was more important, so she kept sewing late into the night. When she finished the last stitch, she snipped off the thread and stared at her handiwork. The horseshoe looked even clumsier than she'd expected, but it was better than nothing.

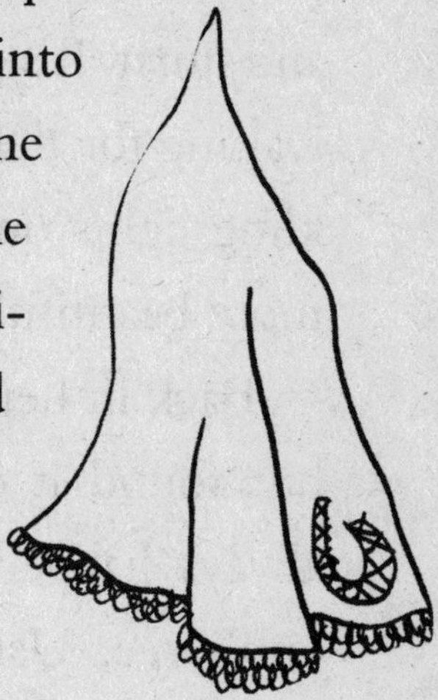

She carefully folded the hankie and wrapped it in beautiful blue paper decorated with more horseshoes, and rosettes. Then she wrote, *To Kate, my best friend in all the world* on the label in gold ink. It wasn't the perfect present, as she'd wanted it to be, but it still looked pretty.

She crept downstairs and put the tiny

parcel beside the large one containing Kate's present for her. The ballroom was empty and quiet. It seemed to be holding its breath, waiting for the Jamboree to start. The twinkling lights on the huge centerpiece looked more beautiful than ever in the darkness.

Back in her room, Ellie jumped into bed but found it difficult to go to sleep. This always happened on the eve of the Royal Jamboree. Usually it was because she was excited, but this year was different. This year she was worried, too. Her plan was so important. What would she do if it didn't work?

Eventually, her tiredness overcame her racing thoughts, and she fell asleep.

When she woke up, light was streaming through the curtains. Immediately, she remembered her wish and bounced out of bed. "Please, please, let there be snow," she pleaded as she opened the curtains. But there wasn't any. The view from her window looked exactly the same as it always did. The sky was clear and blue, without a hint of clouds.

Ellie tried not to feel too disappointed. It wouldn't be too bad if this were the only thing that went wrong today. She would be much more upset, however, if her plan failed.

Chapter 8

Ellie threw her riding clothes on and ran through the silent palace to her parents' room. "Happy Jamboree!" she shouted, as she popped her head around the door. "Any news of my plan?"

"Happy Jamboree to you, too," yawned the King. "We haven't heard anything yet, but I'm sure Higginbottom is doing his best."

"You'll know as soon as he gets back," added the Queen. She sat up in bed, popped her everyday crown on top of her curlers, and gave Ellie a big hug. Then she pulled a parcel from under her pillow and handed it to Ellie. "We thought you might like this now, although all your other presents will have to wait until after the broadcast."

"Thanks!" cried Ellie, as she tore the paper open. Her eyes lit up with delight when she saw the tin of glittering silver hoof polish inside. "That's just what I need for Shadow."

She crumpled up the paper and tossed it into the wastepaper basket. Then she gave her mom and dad a kiss, picked up the hoof polish, and raced down to the stable.

Kate caught up with her just outside the yard. "Look what Grandma gave me!" she cried, waving a chocolate horse-shoe in the air. She snapped it in half, gave one piece to Ellie, and started to eat the remaining piece.

For a little while, they both munched in silence. Then Ellie

asked, "Does your granddad like the outfit that Gloria found for him?"

Kate nodded. "He put it on last night to show us. He looked so funny that he cheered me up a bit." She was quiet for a moment and then added wistfully, "I wish Mom and Dad were here to see him. The Royal Jamboree doesn't feel the same without them."

"I'm sorry," sighed Ellie.

"You'd both better cheer up and get to work," said Meg, as she led Shadow into the yard. "You don't have much time to get him ready, and he's really dirty." The Shetland pony had obviously been lying down during the night. His mane and tail were full of straw, and his legs were covered with dirt.

Ellie and Kate brushed and brushed until

Shadow was completely clean. By the time they had finished, his black coat gleamed in the sunshine, and his long mane and tail were free of tangles. They put on the harness they had decorated the day before. Then they braided silver streamers into his mane, tied a huge silver bow on the top of his tail, and used Ellie's new hoof polish to paint his hooves to match.

Ellie stepped back to admire their work. "He looks fantastic!"

"Gloria Doria will be thrilled," said Kate.

"But my mom and dad won't be thrilled if we're late," added Ellie, glancing at her watch. "We'd better get ourselves ready now."

"I'm looking forward to giving you your present for real," said Kate as they ran back to the side door of the palace.

Ellie gulped. She wasn't really looking forward to giving Kate hers.

Chapter 9

Ellie showered quickly and put on her special Royal Jamboree dress. She wore a new one every year, and her parents always chose it for her. This one was pink, like all her other clothes, and made of shimmery satin decorated with golden ruffles. As soon as she had fastened the zipper, she popped a sparkly tiara on her head, slipped her feet into a pair of gold sandals, and ran down to the ballroom.

It looked even more festive than it had the day before. There was a log fire crackling in the fireplace, gold dishes piled high with sugared almonds, and crystal dishes full of nuts and sweets.

Ellie went to join the crowd gathering near the Jamboree centerpiece; she was surprised to see that the curtains at one end of the room were still closed.

"It's to make sure Shadow is a big surprise," whispered Gloria. "We don't want anyone noticing that the French windows are open until we're ready."

"But how will they see Shadow arrive?" asked Ellie.

"That's your job. When you hear his bells tinkling, I want you and Kate to run over to the window and open the curtains."

Ellie started to walk away. Then she turned back and whispered, "There may be another surprise, too."

"Your father's already told me all about that," Gloria replied with a wink. "If your plan works, it will make the broadcast even better."

By now, it was nearly time for the program to begin. The King was pacing up and down, practicing his speech. Almost everyone else was already in place.

"Have you seen Great-Aunt Edwina?" asked the Queen.

"Er . . . she's not coming," said Ellie. Her mind raced as she struggled to think of a believable excuse. "She's got a headache."

It wasn't a very convincing lie, but it seemed to satisfy the Queen. "Oh, dear," she said. "I do hope she'll be better in time for the Jamboree feast."

A bell rang. "One minute to broadcast," called Gloria. "Places, everyone."

Ellie sat down close to Kate and looked around at the sea of faces. To her disappointment, her great-aunt wasn't the only person missing. Higginbottom was nowhere to be seen. He was a vital part of her plan. If he didn't get back soon, she would know for sure that her plan had completely failed.

"Action!" called Gloria. They all waved at the camera as they'd rehearsed. Then the King stood up and started his speech.

Ellie knew she was supposed to look at him while he was speaking. But her eyes kept straying to the huge double doors that led to the hall. They stayed stubbornly shut. There was still no sign of Higginbottom.

The King stopped talking and sat down. It was now time for the children to exhange their presents. Everyone looked at the girls as Kate thrust her present into Ellie's hands. "Happy Jamboree, Ellie!" she said loudly. Then she added in a whisper, "It's just what you always wanted."

For a brief moment, Ellie wondered if she could put off opening the present so she didn't have to give hers to Kate. Then her excitement got the better of her, and she tore open the wrapping paper.

Inside was a beautiful blouse. It was soft and fluffy, and, best of all, it wasn't pink like Ellie's other clothes. It was a gorgeous pale purple—her favorite color. She put it on right away. It looked strange over her new dress, but it felt wonderful.

"Thank you!" she said. "It's fantastic."

"Now give her yours," whispered the Queen. "Everyone's waiting."

Ellie glanced at the doors again. They were still shut. Dismally, she picked up the tiny parcel she'd wrapped the previous night and handed it to Kate. "Here you go," she said. "I'm sorry it's so small."

Kate read the gold writing on the label and smiled. At that moment, a slight movement attracted Ellie's attention. Her heart skipped a beat as she realized that the double doors were opening. Perhaps there was hope after all. A second later, Higginbottom slipped into the room and gave her a thumbs-up signal.

Kate ripped the paper open and pulled out the small square of white cloth. "It's a hankie," she said, in a slightly surprised voice.

"It's . . . um . . . to cover your eyes," said Ellie. "You must keep them closed until I tell you to open them."

She waited until she was sure her friend wasn't peeking. Then she ran out through the double doors to get Kate's real present.

Chapter 10

In the hallway, Ellie met the two people she most wanted to see. The man was tall, bearded, and suntanned; the woman was shorter, with straight brown hair just like Kate's. They both looked rather nervous at being in the palace.

"I'm so glad to see you," said Ellie. "You're just in time." She took them by the hand and led them to the Jamboree centerpiece in the ballroom. Kate couldn't see them—she was standing with her eyes shut tight and holding the hankie over her face.

Ellie carefully guided the two visitors to a spot right in front of Kate. After fussing over their precise positions for a few moments, she called out to Kate, "You can look now."

Kate lowered the hankie and opened her eyes. Instantly, her face lit up with delight. "Mom! Dad!" she squealed, trying to hug them both at once. "But you said you couldn't get here. I thought you'd missed the last plane."

"We had," said her dad, as he wrapped his arms around her in an enormous hug. "But then Princess Aurelia stepped in to help."

Kate looked at Ellie. "What did you do?"

Ellie grinned. "I talked my mom and dad

into sending the royal jet to get them."
Before she could say any more, she heard the sound of tinkling bells. Immediately, she grabbed Kate by the hand and dragged her toward one end of the room. "Come on, let's see what's outside."

As they pulled the curtains open, Ellie gasped with surprise. Outside the French windows was a blanket of white. Sunlight twinkled on a thick layer of snow that carpeted the palace garden. Icicles hung from the window frames and dripped from the snow-covered branches of the nearby trees. It looked absolutely beautiful.

To make the picture perfect, Shadow trotted into view. He proudly pulled his carriage, as if he knew he was the star of the show. Ellie and Kate's decorations looked fantastic. The stars and silver bells made the carriage sparkle. Shadow's mane and tail sparkled, too. The silver leaves on his bridle bobbed gently every time his glittery hooves touched the ground.

Great-Aunt Edwina smiled happily as she held the reins. Her silk dress and wide-brimmed hat were trimmed with silver to match the carriage. Beside her sat the most enormous squirrel Ellie had ever seen. It was a brilliant costume. She would never have guessed it was Kate's granddad inside if she hadn't known already.

As Shadow trotted into the ballroom, they

both waved and shouted, "Happy Jamboree!"

Everyone waved back. Then they crowded excitedly around the carriage to get a better view of the new arrivals.

The King waved happily at the nearest camera. "Here's wishing everyone a wonderful Jamboree!" he declared, as everyone cheered and clapped.

"Cut!" called Gloria. "Well done! That

was the perfect end to a brilliant broadcast."

"And what a wonderful surprise!" said the Queen.

Kate put her arms around Ellie and hugged her. "Thanks a million. You've given me the perfect present."

"That's what friends are for," said Ellie. "But there's one thing I don't understand. Where did all that snow come from?"

Gloria winked at her and laughed. "Sometimes wishes need a bit of help from the special-effects team."

"Wow!" said Ellie. "It looks so real."

She took a peppermint from one of the crystal dishes and gave it to Shadow. While he munched on it, she looked at Kate, smiling happily as she snuggled close to her parents. She looked at the sparkling carriage.

And she looked at the snow.

"This is definitely the best Royal Jamboree I've ever had," she announced. "Wishes sometimes *do* come true."